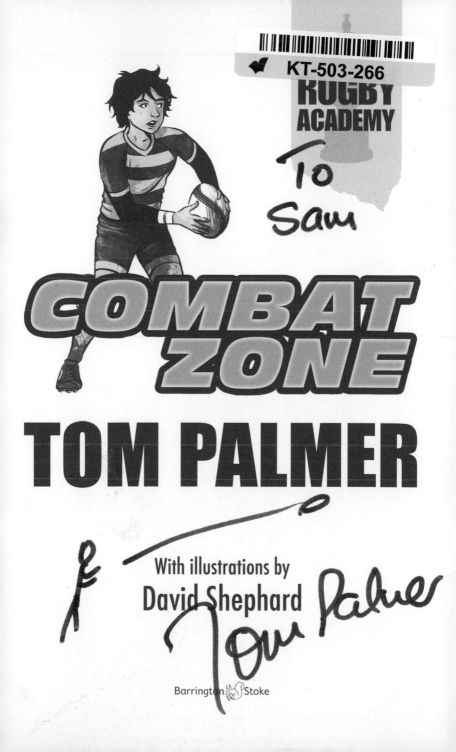

RUGBY
ACADEMY

To Sam

COMBAT ZONE

TOM PALMER

With illustrations by
David Shephard

Barrington Stoke

First published in 2014 in Great Britain by
Barrington Stoke Ltd
18 Walker Street, Edinburgh, EH3 7LP

www.barringtonstoke.co.uk

Text © 2014 Tom Palmer
Illustrations © 2014 David Shephard

A CIP catalogue record for this book is available
from the British Library upon request

ISBN: 978-1-78112-397-3

Printed in China by Leo

For the children and adults at
Albrighton Primary School and at RAF Cosford,
with thanks for their help.

ONE

The silver BMW made a sharp swerve left to avoid the deer that stood frozen in its headlights. Woody held his breath. A part of him wished the car had come off the road. But only so that the journey would stop – he didn't have a death wish or anything like that.

But the car didn't come off the road. Woody watched his dad's arms tense as he controlled the car with perfect skill. That was how Woody's dad always drove. It was part of who he was.

A man who liked to travel at speed.

A fighter pilot in the RAF.

Woody stared out of the car window. Its headlights lit up the forest on either side of the road. Thick tree-trunks flashed by.

"I don't want to do this," Woody said. "I liked my old school. I liked my friends. I'm just about to start my GCSEs."

His dad didn't take his eyes from the road. "Borderlands is a great school," he said. "It was my school. You'll make new friends. You'll play lots of sport."

"The wrong sport," Woody snapped.

His dad paused before he spoke again. Woody knew he was working out what to say so that he could win the argument.

"Rugby is a wonderful game," his dad said at last. "I learned more from rugby than you'll ever learn playing soccer. And the school runs a serious rugby academy now."

"It's called football," Woody said. "And I like football. I'm good at football. You know I am."

Woody's dad was silent again. They were out of the forest now. The BMW was speeding up a winding slope onto a moor.

Woody thought about the letter he had received a month before, from Norwich City. They'd offered him a place in their football academy. That was the reason his dad was driving him to Borderlands – to stop him being a footballer. Woody had even had to hide his football in his bag, so his dad didn't know he'd taken it with him.

"There's more to life than sport," his dad went on. "You'll get a better education at Borderlands. It's a fine school. One of the best."

Woody didn't reply. He wanted to swear at his dad like his dad swore when he was angry. But Woody kept his anger locked deep inside himself. It was at times like this that he wished his mum was still around. She always knew how to break the tension. But she was in Australia. Remarried with two new daughters. Woody had made the choice to stay in England with his dad.

After a few minutes of tense silence, Woody's dad switched on the radio. The news headlines filled the car.

Floods in Cornwall and Devon.

The Man U manager had been sacked.

Then back to the main story.

"There have been further scenes of violent conflict in the Central Asian Republic," the reporter said. "The Prime Minister is on his way to New York to speak at the United Nations. Before he left, he said, 'We must take this situation seriously. It threatens the peace of the whole Middle East. We must do what we can for the people of the Central Asian

Republic.' Experts predict that the UK will be at war within 24 hours."

Woody saw his dad's hands tighten their grip on the steering wheel.

TWO

"Wow!" Woody's mouth fell open. He couldn't help it. He'd seen photos of his dad's old school, but it still took his breath away in real life.

It was nothing like Woody's last school. That didn't have a high stone wall all around it. It didn't have a mile-long, tree-lined drive leading to its front door, either.

But what struck Woody most was in front of the school, in pride of place. A rugby field, lit up by four massive floodlights. On the pitch behind it he saw 20 or so boys in blue and yellow striped shirts.

"That's Luxton Park. The hallowed turf," Woody's dad said. "Magnificent, isn't it?"

"It's very nice, Dad," Woody said. He had decided not to argue any more. In the three minutes it had taken to travel up the school drive, he'd made a plan. A plan that would solve all his problems.

Woody's dad smiled as he parked in front of the school.

"This brings back memories," he said.

"Yeah?"

"Oh yes." Woody's dad leaned back in his seat to stretch his back and shoulders. "Of course, your grandad sent me up on the train."

As they spoke, a light came on outside the school and a man appeared at the car window.

"Flight Officer Woodward?" the man said. "We've been expecting you. I'm Mr Clayton."

Mr Clayton was a little older than Woody's dad. He had short dark hair that was just turning grey.

"Good evening," Woody's dad said. "This is …"

"I get called Woody," Woody said.

"Hello, Woody," Mr Clayton said. "I'm going to be your housemaster at Borderlands. I'm here to help you with anything and everything."

"Thank you," Woody said.

"May I speak to your father for a moment?"

Woody nodded. His dad got out of the car, giving Woody a chance to look at a road map in the door pocket. He tried to listen in on what his dad and Mr Clayton were saying, but the sound of dozens of rugby boots on concrete drowned their words out.

After a couple of minutes, Woody's dad signalled to Woody to get out of the car.

"Right. I'll be off," he announced. "Long drive back to Lincolnshire."

"See you, Dad," Woody said with a grin. He could tell his dad was surprised that he was so calm about being left at Borderlands. But it was clear he was pleased too – he had never been fond of goodbyes.

Of course, he didn't know about Woody's plan.

Mr Clayton led Woody down a wood-panelled corridor and across a stone courtyard into another building.

"You're sharing a room with two other boys," he explained. "Owen and Rory. Nice lads. They're keen on rugby, too."

"Thank you," Woody said. He didn't see much reason to point out that he wasn't keen on rugby.

"And I meant what I told you," Mr Clayton said. "If I can help you with anything, please say."

Mr Clayton knocked on a door, then led Woody into the room, where two boys were sitting on their beds. One was reading. The other was typing on a laptop. They both jumped up and grinned.

When the housemaster had gone, Owen put the kettle on.

"What did you bring?" he asked. "We've got hot chocolate and biscuits. Want some? I'll make it while you unpack."

Woody nodded. "Yes please," he said. He knew he needed to take on as much food as he could – it was going to be a long night. He also knew he wasn't going to unpack.

After they'd drunk their hot chocolate and eaten two packets of biscuits, Woody decided to tell Owen and Rory his plan. They were getting

on well and he felt it would be wrong not to. He couldn't just disappear. He felt kind of sad he would only know the two boys for the next hour or two.

"Listen," he said. "I'm planning to leave tonight."

"Leave?" Owen stared at him.

Woody explained his plan to run across the hills to a train station about 14 miles away. He'd checked the map in the car. He'd sleep in the station for the rest of the night, get the first train to Birmingham in the morning, then head on to Lincolnshire.

"But won't your dad just bring you back?" Rory asked.

Woody shook his head. "I think he'll understand that I'm not happy. If I'm home by breakfast."

THREE

Woody waited until midnight before he set off.

All that he had with him was a small rucksack with a change of clothes, a bottle of water and another packet of biscuits that Rory had given him.

He jogged across the school rugby pitch, warming his legs up for a long night of running. But then he was surprised by a beam of light that came from behind him and swept across the grass.

On instinct, he speeded up into a sprint.

"Hey! I can see you out there," a voice shouted. "Keep off our property. This is a school, not a public park. I'm releasing the dog."

A bark. A rush of adrenaline. Woody ran harder.

The high stone wall was right ahead. Woody sprinted towards it, not convinced he could scale it. The drop on the other side would be well over two metres.

But Woody had no choice. If he didn't get over the wall, he'd get bitten by the dog, and his escape attempt would be over. He ran. Hard. He made the wall, scaled it, lay on the top, then dropped down as softly as he could.

Woody landed on both feet, bending his knees. He paused and held his breath. It was OK. A safe landing. No more sounds of man or dog.

Now to run into the hills.

The night was dark away from Borderlands, but Woody knew which road to follow – it was the same one his dad had driven him along. The run out of the town and up the valley was fine. Woody had done night-running along the river at home and he was used to the sounds of the night as he ran. But up on the moors it was different. The sky was huge, filled with a million pinprick stars. And it was quiet. Woody felt lonely and small in that huge open space. He couldn't help but wonder if this was how his dad felt when he was alone in his plane in the night sky.

The rest of the night went to plan. But when Woody got off the train in his home town at 8.30 the next morning, he noticed that there were more fighter aircraft in the sky than he had ever seen before. Tiny silver reflections of sunlight high above the miles upon miles of the flat fields of Lincolnshire.

A Typhoon took off from the airbase, its engines firing, the air vibrating.

But perhaps this was normal. When the British Prime Minister was at the United Nations the RAF would step up their training. It looked good on the news. It sent the message that the UK was ready to send its air force into action.

Woody walked along the lane to his home, hands in pockets, lost in thought. At the front door he knocked, rather than letting himself into the house and giving his dad a fright.

There was no reply.

And Woody realised that something didn't feel right. His dad always did the same things at the same time and right now he should be out of the shower, eating his breakfast, hungry after his morning run. Then Woody noticed the BMW wasn't in the garage. And the bins were out in the road, even though it wasn't bin day.

Woody fished his iPhone out of his rucksack. There was a message.

> Woody. We've been
> mobilised. Short notice.
> I'll phone when I can. Try
> and enjoy school. Love
> Dad

Woody sat down on the doorstep. Then he threw up.

When he had recovered, Woody flicked through the BBC News app on his phone.

The Prime Minister was back in the UK. Parliament would vote that day on whether to go to war to secure the stability of the Central Asian Republic. Woody knew what would happen. They would vote yes.

The rest of the world might not know there was going to be a war, but the RAF was already on its way.

FOUR

Back at Borderlands, Woody was sitting on his bed when the door to the dorm burst open. It was Owen and Rory, both in blue and yellow tops and covered in mud.

Rory came over, put his rugby ball on the floor and shook Woody's hand. Then he picked the ball back up and began to collect flecks of cut grass off the carpet, one by one.

"Training," Owen explained. "First XV."

"Right," Woody said.

"How was the escape?" Owen asked.

Woody smiled. "I made it all the way home."

"How was your dad?" Rory asked.

Woody wasn't sure what to say and for a moment the three boys looked at each other in uncomfortable silence. Then Rory spotted the pack of blueys on Woody's bed – official RAF postcards families could send to personnel who were away in combat.

Rory screwed up his face. "I'm sorry. He's gone, hasn't he?"

A wave of panic stopped Woody from speaking. It was the same panic he'd felt on the step at home. He took a deep breath and looked out of the window at a groundsman who was replacing divots on the rugby pitch.

"David's dad's gone too," Owen said. "You've not met David yet. And Jesse – he's David's mate – his dad's an Air Marshal. He's gone too.

There are a quite few boys here whose parents have gone."

Woody had been ten the last time his dad had been deployed. Back then, it had been exciting. His dad was a fighter pilot. One of the best airmen in the world. His mum had been at home then, and she had helped him to stay positive about the fact his dad was gone. Woody had been proud, not worried about what could go wrong. Now he'd prefer it if his dad was a groundsman, like the one outside.

"Listen," Owen said. "We're going to watch the match now. Rory's got an Australian pay-TV channel. Australia's playing New Zealand. Want to watch it with us?"

Woody nodded. It was a good plan. A way of not having to talk.

Australia against New Zealand was a fierce encounter. The two teams battered each other from kick-off. An Australian was taken off for a bleeding cut after 8 minutes. A Kiwi after 12.

Woody watched with mixed feelings. He loved to see players running hard with the ball, smashing through a tackle, or being brought down. But the scrums sent a shiver up his spine. Anything could happen in that pile of bodies. He watched as a huge man was dragged under a scrum. He was two metres tall at least, but still he ended up tipped up so that his legs were in the air.

It reminded Woody of a player he'd seen at a match once, with his dad at their local ground. The scrum had collapsed and when everyone stood back up, one man was still lying there. He was carried off the pitch on a stretcher.

Woody had only been five at the time and he'd thought the player had died and was being taken away to be put in a coffin. It had worried him so much that he couldn't get to sleep that night, so he'd gone into his parents' room to ask his dad about it. His dad said the man was only knocked out, not dead.

From then on, Woody had never wanted to play rugby. He couldn't shake off the chill of fear he'd felt as a 5-year-old boy.

But he said nothing about that to Owen and Rory. He just drank his Coke and – he had to be honest with himself – kind of enjoyed the match.

FIVE

"Do you fancy a school tour, now you're staying?" Rory asked.

"OK," Woody said. "You're on."

Owen, Rory and Woody walked down endless corridors, past classrooms, a dining hall, and random piles of sports kit. Owen introduced Woody to several other boys as they walked. Most were friendly and shook Woody's hand.

But then he met two Borderlands pupils who weren't friendly in the least. A tall boy with light hair and a sneer, and his shorter, stockier friend.

"Who's this?" the light-haired boy asked Owen.

"This is Woody," Owen said, in a guarded tone. "Woody, this is Jesse and David."

"Hi," Woody said, and put his hand out.

There was a moment of silence. Then Jesse and David just walked on down the corridor.

Woody was confused. He rubbed his forehead. "What's their problem?" he asked.

"They're tricky," Owen replied. "Especially Jesse. He's worth keeping an eye out for."

"What do you mean?" Woody asked.

"He can be ..." Rory hesitated. "... Difficult."

Woody tried to look like he understood, but he didn't. They reached a common room next. A big TV was on, showing the news. Woody felt compelled to watch.

The reporter was saying that the RAF was already over the Central Asian Republic, where they could monitor developments in the troubled country. And Typhoons were moving in from Cyprus, ready to attack if needed.

Woody shuddered. The thought of his dad in his Typhoon made him shake with fear. Fear that he might be called into action like he had been over Iraq, Afghanistan and Libya. He hated the idea. His dad alone in a red hot sky, while surface-to-air missiles rocketed towards him.

"Good evening, boys."

The voice at the door made the boys jump. A female voice. The head teacher, Mrs Page.

Owen, Rory and Woody stood up straight away, as did several other boys. Someone pressed mute on the TV remote control. This was the first time Woody had seen the head teacher up close. She looked like she meant business in her smart trouser suit. Mr Clayton was with her.

"I know you boys have an interest in the war," Mrs Page said. "But don't watch too much of it on the news. The reporters' job isn't just to inform their viewers, it's also to entertain them. And that means they don't always stick to the truth. Do you understand?"

"Yes, Miss," Rory and Owen said.

"I hope you're settling in, Woodward?" Mrs Page asked.

"Er ... yes, Miss," Woody felt himself blushing under the head teacher's gaze. Did she know about last night? His escape?

"Woodward is settling in very well," Mr Clayton said.

"Good." Mrs Page turned to leave. "And remember what I said about the TV news, boys."

"Yes, Miss," Woody said again.

When Mrs Page had gone, Woody nodded to Mr Clayton. "Thank you," he said. "I owe you a favour, sir."

"Indeed you do." Mr Clayton rubbed his hands together. "Which is good, because I need one."

Woody smiled and waited to hear what Mr Clayton wanted from him.

"Mr Johnson is short of players," Mr Clayton said. "He needs backs. And you look like a back to me, Woody."

"A back as in rugby, sir?" Woody asked.

"Yes, rugby," Mr Clayton said. He picked up the remote and switched off the TV. "Mr Johnson is the rugby master and I think it's time you met him."

SIX

"What do you do after dinner?" Woody asked, as he and Owen and Rory walked away from the dining hall later that evening.

"Homework," Owen replied. "I'm going to the library. It's quiet now. Miss Evans will be there on her own."

"I'll come with you," Woody said. "I need a library right now."

Rory tapped each wooden panel as they walked along the corridor. Woody didn't comment on it. He was getting used to Rory's funny habits.

"I need to practise kicking," Rory said. "Before it gets dark."

Rory disappeared down a corridor to the pitches outside, and Woody and Owen walked on to the library. Owen took Woody in and they went up to the desk.

"This is Woody," Owen said. "He needs some help."

"Great. Hello, Woody – I'm Miss Evans," the librarian said. "What can I do to help?"

Woody looked at Miss Evans. She had bright, happy-looking eyes and was wearing a Welsh rugby top. 'Is everyone in this school obsessed with rugby?' he thought. But he kept his thoughts to himself.

"I need a book on the rules of rugby, please," Woody said.

Miss Evans led Woody to the sports books. He was surprised to see a whole shelf of books on how to play rugby.

"There are loads," he said. "I never thought there'd be so many."

"There are loads," Miss Evans agreed. "And they're all useful. But you want this one."

Woody took the book. It was called *Know the Game: Rugby Union*. He hoped it did what it said on the cover. He loved sport, but he still felt reluctant to play rugby. Very reluctant. But he had made Mr Clayton a promise. And he reckoned it was a promise the housemaster wouldn't let him break.

Woody found a comfy seat and opened the book.

He read about the dimensions of a Rugby Union pitch. The size of the ball. The positions of the players. Forwards in the scrum. Backs lined out behind them.

Woody frowned. He'd always thought the backs went in the scrum. He had a lot to learn.

As Woody read, he heard the library door open and close and random footsteps come in and out, but he was too engrossed to look up. Miss Evans had been right about this book. Now he was reading about ways to score. Five points for a try. Two for a conversion. Three for a drop goal or penalty.

All of a sudden there was a hand on the table in front of him. Knuckles white, nails bitten down.

Woody looked up and saw Jesse and David looming over him.

"What's that you're reading?" Jesse asked.

"It's a book about rugby." Woody knew the boys weren't being friendly, but he grinned at them anyway.

Jesse smiled a nasty smile. "A book about rugby? Are you serious?"

Woody did his best to smile again. But he said nothing.

"That's the kind of thing I'd expect David's kid sister to do," Jesse went on. "You don't learn about rugby in a book. You learn it on the pitch."

Woody looked at David. Now he looked angry with Jesse. Owen hadn't been kidding when he said Jesse was difficult.

SEVEN

Woody had never felt so awkward. A gum shield was pushing his lips out and he had a scrum cap squashing his head. Rugby gear. He'd never needed all this stuff to play football. It made him worry even more about getting hurt. But he had a promise to keep.

Woody stuck close to Rory and Owen, who led him to a pitch on the far side of the school grounds.

"Why aren't we training on there?" Woody asked, looking across at Luxton Park. He'd been looking forward to telling his dad he'd played on the "hallowed turf".

Owen laughed and looked at Rory. "If you go on there Mr Johnson will have to kill you."

"What?"

"First XV games only. Nobody else is allowed on there – except the groundsman."

Woody shook his head. This school was weird.

A giant of a man was leading the training, assisted by another man who had a permanent scowl.

Owen and Rory told Woody who the coaches were as they walked over towards them. The giant was the chief coach, Mr Johnson. The scowler was his assistant, Mr Searle. Woody also noticed three figures passing fast balls to one another at close range. Jesse, David and another boy, Thomas. Owen had introduced Woody to him earlier.

The sight of Jesse made Woody feel even more uneasy. He watched Jesse as he spoke to the other two and pointed at Woody. All three of them started laughing. Woody felt a heat run up the back of his neck, into his head. He knew this feeling – it was anger. The same as his dad's anger. His dad's voice came to him – "Always channel the red mist, Woody."

Woody decided to follow his dad's advice. He had his anger. He had his worries about rugby. He had his fears for his dad. And he needed a way to channel those angers and fears that didn't involve running away again. He'd do it by throwing himself into the game.

Training began – under floodlights while a halo of rain drifted across the pitch.

First they jogged the lengths of the pitch and then, once they were warmed up, they sprinted widths. Woody made sure he finished ahead of everyone else at each sprint. He might not know how to play rugby, but he did know how to run.

Next they practised passing in lines up and down the pitch. After one length of the pitch, Mr Johnson stopped the session and walked up to Woody.

"Spin it," he said.

"Sorry, sir?"

"The ball. When you pass, spin it." The coach gave the ball back to Woody. "I'm Mr Johnson," he said. "You must be Woodward?"

"I am, sir."

"He's not got to the bit in the book about passing yet," Woody heard Jesse shout over.

Mr Johnson looked at Jesse, then Woody, waiting for someone to explain.

"I've not played much rugby," Woody admitted. "I don't know how to spin the ball."

Mr Johnson nodded, then showed Woody what to do. "If you spin it," he explained, "the ball will travel further and you can control it better."

Then he jogged backwards and tossed the ball to Woody. Woody saw the ball spinning, as it moved in a straight line towards him. He tossed it back, trying to spin it too. After three or four goes, he started to feel like he had control of the ball.

"Good," Mr Johnson said. "You're a natural."

After passing, they worked on charging.

One boy took the ball from a short pass, then ran at another two boys, who were holding blue and yellow tackle pads. The idea was for the attacker to make ground by hitting the defenders hard.

Woody stood in line. As he waited he tried to spin the ball, practising what Mr Johnson had shown him, tossing it upwards.

"Spinning the ball is on page 32 of *Rugby for Idiots*," Woody heard Jesse say in a slow, stupid-sounding voice.

One or two other boys laughed.

Woody felt his anger rising again, just as it was his turn to go.

He tossed the ball to Mr Johnson, then began to run, taking a short pass back from the coach. Then he accelerated. Fast. He charged at three boys with yellow and blue pads. He hit them. Hard. Really hard. It hurt – for a second. Then there was a rush of adrenaline, and he felt the defenders give to the weight of his shoulder. It felt good.

After training, Mr Johnson walked alongside Woody. He was at least a head taller than Woody and twice as wide across the shoulders.

Both his ears stuck out, like he'd spent a lifetime in the scrum.

"Fast, aren't you?" he asked.

"I suppose," Woody said.

"You've not played rugby before?"

"Football. I was a centre forward." Woody wondered if he should say that Norwich City wanted him, but he decided he would sound like he was showing off if he did.

"At a high level, I bet?" the coach said. "Your acceleration is remarkable."

"Thank you, sir," Woody said.

"Listen," Mr Johnson said. "We've lost a couple of lads. Brothers. Backs. I might be able to use you in the teams. If we trained you up."

Woody nodded.

"You'd need to put in a lot of work," Mr Johnson warned.

Woody thought of his dad. How funny it would be to tell him that he was in one of the rugby teams at school. And that he had even enjoyed the training session.

"I'll put the work in," Woody said. "Sir."

EIGHT

Woody's iPad flashed to Skype just after he'd got into bed and picked up his rugby book.

His dad. He felt a rush of excitement.

"Dad! How are you? Where are you?"

"Fine, son. How's Borderlands?"

Woody understood. His dad couldn't answer his questions. He wasn't allowed to say anything about where he was and what he was doing. There was a war on – and he was fighting in it.

"Great," Woody said.

He watched his dad's face relax.

"Friends?" he asked.

"I'm in with two lads," Woody told him. "They're sound."

Woody glanced at his room-mates. Rory was scribbling in a notebook. Owen was on his Xbox.

"How's the schoolwork?" Dad asked.

"Not done much yet," Woody said. "But I'm on the team."

"Oh, don't tell me they play soccer now," his dad sighed. "That's the end."

"Rugby, Dad."

"What?"

"I did rugby training. It went well. The coach wants to work with me."

His dad looked stunned. Woody felt a wave
of happiness, then sadness. He didn't want
to give in to his confused feelings, so he fired
another question at his dad.

"How's the war?"

"You know I can't talk about it, Wood. I'm
fine. Busy. I only have another minute or two."

"I know," Woody said. That was how
these calls always were. Short. Intense.
Unsatisfying.

"Look, I've been worried," Dad went on.
"The way I bundled you off to Borderlands. So,
I wanted to make you a deal. To make it easier
while you're there and I'm here."

"Go on."

"You throw yourself into it there – enjoy it –
and when I get back we'll talk about where you
want to be. OK?"

"That sounds fair," Woody said. "It's a deal."

He knew his dad was worried. But he also knew his dad had to give his job 100%. A fighter pilot couldn't be worrying about his son and if he liked his school or not. He needed all his focus to survive. But, still, Woody couldn't resist one last question.

"And we'll talk about what sport I want to play?" he asked.

There was a pause.

Then his dad smiled and said, "Yes, that too."

An hour later, Woody was outside in the courtyard. It was raining, and he was pleased. He was less likely to be disturbed in the rain.

He dropped his football on the stone slabs and trapped it. For a moment he didn't kick it. He was thinking about what his dad was doing now. Woody imagined him putting his flying gear on, his helmet, then walking across the runway to his plane. He would check the aircraft's wings, wheels, cannons – and then climb in.

Woody stopped imagining there, and fired the football hard at a wall. It bounced back and he left-foot controlled it, then hit it with his right. He did this over and over, harder and harder, till sweat ran down his back. The effort felt really good. The more he put in, the less he had to think about his dad. About anything. Woody didn't want to think at all. Just kick, kick, kick.

"HEY YOU!" The voice was sharp and loud.

Woody trapped his football and turned round. Mr Searle was at the door, hands on hips. Woody watched him, unsure of what to do.

"Give me that ball," Mr Searle demanded.

Woody flicked the ball up with his instep, walked over to the coach and handed it to him.

"You're new, so I'll let this go," Mr Searle growled. "But this is a rugby school. No soccer balls." Then he turned and marched towards the sports building, the football under his arm.

Woody felt a flash of rage. What about his football?

"When do I get the ball back?" Woody shouted. "SIR?"

"You don't," Mr Searle said, not looking round.

No way!

How unfair could you get?

Woody watched Mr Searle go in a door and a light come on. He heard excited yapping. It was the dog from the night he tried to escape. Of course – it had been Mr Searle with the torch that night.

Woody approached and peered in through a metal grille at a window. He could see Mr Searle with the football in one hand. And, in the other hand, a pair of shears. Woody watched him put the ball on the ground, lift the shears high, then plunge them down to stab the football. The dog was leaping around the room, barking and snapping. Finally, Mr Searle threw the punctured ball to the dog. It set on it as if it was a small animal to kill.

Now Woody's anger was off the scale.

But he could do nothing. Not to the dog. Not to Mr Searle. So he ran. Across Luxton Park, then around the perimeter wall. He would run until he was sick or he collapsed. He felt the strain in his legs first. Then his lungs. And then the feeling of power began to overcome his anger.

NINE

A couple of weeks passed. Woody did Maths,
English, even Latin. He tried hard and kept out
of trouble. He was aware that the school would
report back to parents about boys' progress.
Woody didn't want his dad to think that he was
going back on their deal. He would tolerate
Borderlands until the war was over.

In the Central Asian Republic, British planes
were still bombing rebel air fields, defences and
other key targets. The south of the country
and its borders were safe now and the RAF was
turning its attention to the north. This meant
more danger for pilots like Woody's dad.

On the rugby field, Woody threw himself
into every training session. He went out at

other times with Owen and Rory to practise his skills. He had overcome his fear of hurting himself.

Yes, you fell over.

Yes, you bashed into people or they bashed into you.

Yes, other boys piled on top of you and pushed you this way and that.

But you came out laughing, rather than crying. The pain you felt on impact gave way fast to adrenaline and the thrill of being part of a team. It felt good to be playing a sport that involved something close to wrestling, using your strength and your skill to get the better of someone else. Woody liked it – and he thought he was pretty good at it, too.

And Mr Johnson was happy with him.

During one practice game, Woody made Mr Johnson even happier. It was the First

XV versus the Second XV. A warm up for the Firsts, who were due to play a semi-final in a week's time. And not just any semi-final – the semi-final of the National Schools Trophy. Even Woody knew that it was a big deal.

Woody was in the Seconds.

Twenty minutes into the game, Woody ran from deep, built up pace and received the ball from the scrum half. He wanted to gain a few metres, get closer to the line, and he charged. As he accelerated, he saw no gap between the First XV backs. It was a solid line of boys. So Woody did something he'd read about in his rugby books. He dropped the ball, tapped a grubber kick low, then ran at the First XV line. And all of a sudden he was in space, on his own, un-tackled. The ball bounced ahead of him, the defence were behind him. He kicked it again, over the 22 metre line.

Woody ran at pace, his lungs and legs working hard. Another kick. Softer this time.

He saw the ball bounce once, then twice, then it reared up just before the try line. Woody dived after it, his arms at full stretch.

Contact.

A try.

Woody's first ever try. It felt great, brilliant – nothing like scoring a goal in football. To be on the end of a move, to battle your way past all those other players who were trying to stop you, and then to dive down to put the ball over the line. It made Woody feel like he wanted more. To train and practise and compete as hard as he could, to have that feeling again.

After training, Mr Johnson took Woody aside. "You're doing well," he said. "Very well."

"Thank you, sir."

"I want to take you to the semi-final," Mr Johnson said. "On the bench. Can you cope with that?"

Woody was stunned. Was Mr Johnson really asking him to play for Borderlands in the National Schools Trophy? For the Firsts?

"Am I experienced enough, sir?" he said in disbelief.

Mr Johnson grinned at him. "No."

"Oh," Woody said. He didn't know whether to grin back.

"But I can use you," Mr Johnson told him. "As an impact player. You're a natural sportsman. OK?"

Woody just about managed to say, "Yes."

TEN

When the minibus turned onto the drive of Thornton School in Yorkshire, Woody's heart started to pound.

Until then he had managed to distract himself by joking about with some of the other boys and listening to loud music, but now the scale of what was about to happen struck him. He was on the bench in a rugby game. A high-stakes rugby game. If Borderlands won this game, then they were in the final of the National Schools Trophy.

When Mr Johnson stopped the bus at the top of the school drive, nobody spoke or moved. There was no messing about or pushing to get off. Woody knew it was time for a team talk.

"First of all," Mr Johnson said, "I want you to remember that you represent Borderlands. In everything you do, on and off the field. You will be polite. You will be sporting. You will be grateful. You will be helpful. OK?"

"Yes, sir," they said.

"Second," Mr Johnson went on. "You do everything you can to win this game. Play within the rules, but remember you are 80 minutes away from the final at Twickenham, the home of English rugby. Do you want that?"

"Yes," a few boys said.

"I'm sorry?" Mr Johnson yelled.

"YES!" the whole squad shouted. The minibus shook to the sound of their voices.

The match was tight. The game was locked in the middle third of the muddy pitch. Woody found it hard to tell his own squad from the other team's players for the mud. Two things struck him, sitting so close to the action. One was the smell of the mud. He could really smell it. It reminded him of playing football in the wet. The other was the shouting. Both sets of players – and their coaches – shouted to each other, worked as a unit, communicated non-stop. Woody liked it. And he wanted to be part of it.

Halfway through the second half, the score was 12–12. Four penalties to each team. No tries. Rory had scored four out of his four kicks. The Thornton fly half had scored four from seven.

One boy who was easy to spot was Jesse. He was superb. He dominated the game from scrum half, feeding players the ball, then taking it back, side-stepping tackles. He was an amazing rugby player.

But Woody could see, too, that Borderlands were getting tired. Thornton were gaining more and more ground, which meant they were within kicking distance of the posts if they were to try for a drop goal or if Borderlands gave them a penalty. Woody felt pleased with himself – he was learning to read the game.

Just then he felt a tap on his back. Mr Johnson.

"Warm up," the coach said.

"What?" Woody asked, startled.

"Start warming up," Mr Johnson said. "You're going on in five."

Borderlands had just won a scrum when Woody was sent onto the pitch. He took up position at centre, 15 metres left of Jesse.

At first, Woody struggled to take in the game around him. He knew he had to focus, work with the rest of the team, not give in to his feelings of anxiety. Jesse, hands on the ball, gave Woody a hard stare.

"Watch me," Jesse shouted. "Do what I say. Get the ball to Thomas, to Owen. And listen to the others. Got it?"

"Got it," Woody shouted back.

But Woody had other orders from Mr Johnson. When the ball was fed out to him, he was to run at the Thornton defence. He was to gather pace and hit them hard. Use his power and size to batter them. He was to gain ground by running at and through Thornton.

Woody spotted Thornton's captain shouting at his backs and pointing at Woody. They were wary of him. His fresh legs. The determination on his face. They didn't know he was as green as a rugby player comes.

Jesse fed the ball into the scrum. Seconds later it came out of the back. Jesse waited as the two sets of players pushed at each other. Then he picked the ball up and passed it across the field.

Woody saw the ball come through three sets of hands – Jesse, Thomas and Owen – as the Thornton backs pressed. He had chosen to stay far back to give himself the chance to build momentum with his run. So when the ball came to him he was already running fast. He took it two-handed and close to his side and ran low and hard at the defence. He pushed a hand into the face of his first tackler, deflecting him. Then two players hit him at the same time – one on his legs, one round his hips. Woody crashed to the ground. He'd made seven metres. He turned over and held the ball behind him. Jesse was there, ready to take it.

The last ten minutes of the match felt like an hour to Woody. Every time he got the ball, he did as the coach had told him. Gathered pace. Gained ground. Hit the defence hard. And he did it time after time.

Now Borderlands were making ground. They were less vulnerable to penalties and drop goals. Mr Johnson's plan was working.

The score remained at 12–12.

Woody did his best to put a little bit more into each of his charges. To get stronger with each, not weaker. On his 8th charge one of the other team grabbed him around the neck. The referee's whistle went straight away. High tackle. Dangerous play.

Woody stood when he was free of the heap of bodies that had fallen on top of him. He could see that Rory was holding the ball, eyeing the goals.

The Borderlands team backed off as Rory lined up the kick. The players and the small crowd went quiet. There was just the sound of a flag flapping in the wind. Rory stepped up, moved back two paces, one sideward, his eyes on the posts, then the ball, then the posts again.

One step. Two steps. The sound of boot on ball, as it sailed between the posts. Dead centre. Perfect.

Thornton 12. Borderlands 15.

ELEVEN

Borderlands had won. They were in the final of the National Schools Trophy. At Twickenham. It was beyond belief.

The mood on the minibus was upbeat and excited. Thornton School had given them a huge hamper of cans of Coke, sandwiches, cakes and fruit for the journey home. They ate. They drank. They talked. They laughed. They lived every move and kick of the game again and again.

After an hour, half the boys were bursting for the toilet and the rest wanted to stretch their legs after the game. Their muscles were stiffening, every minor injury nagging.

"Are we nearly there yet?" David joked. He got a few laughs, led by Jesse.

They were halfway across a moor, in the middle of nowhere. Mr Johnson parked the minibus.

"Let's stop here for five minutes, lads," he said. "Take a comfort break. Do some stretching."

Woody heard the minibus radio playing Nirvana as he stumbled in the dark, away from the bus. He stretched his legs and his back as he walked. His shoulders were sore and bruised. But it felt good, like war wounds. He'd earned them.

Then the music stopped. There were voices on the radio now. Woody approached a cluster of his team-mates around the minibus. They all stood in silence.

"What's up?" Woody called out.

"Shhhhh," Owen hissed.

Woody felt his stomach lurch.

"The RAF has made a number of successful strikes around the city of Lusa today," the reporter was saying. "Pairs of Tornados and Typhoons attacked rebel positions while, on the ground ..."

Woody swallowed. Typhoons. This was not how he wanted to hear news about the war. He wanted to be in his room, on his own, so that he could think properly.

"In a separate action in the south of the Central Asian Republic, a British Hercules aircraft has been reported missing," the reporter went on. "The aircraft was on a mission to rescue stranded British oil workers. First reports say it was shot down while attempting to land in the desert ..."

Woody noticed several boys fumble for their mobile phones. Their faces lit up on the dark hillside as they checked for messages.

"Come on, boys," Mr Johnson said. "Into the bus. Let's get back to school."

TWELVE

The first thing Woody did when he woke in the half light of the next morning was to check the BBC News app.

The RAF Hercules had crash-landed before it reached the stranded oil workers. It seemed almost certain that it had been shot down. RAF Search and Rescue had gone straight in and found all four of the crew. Three were injured. One had been killed. His family had been informed. The missions of the other RAF planes involved had been successful.

Woody closed his eyes. He hated this. He wished again that his dad did a nice, safe job like a groundsman – anything other than a fighter pilot.

At breakfast, Woody could sense a gathering gloom. Boys sat at rows of tables with food in front of them, but no one was eating. No one was speaking.

When all the boarders and staff were in the dining hall, Mrs Page stood up. She cleared her throat. "Boys," she said. "We want to speak to you all together. To say this to every one of you."

Woody knew what was coming. The crew member killed on the Hercules. He was connected to Borderlands.

"David Henson left school early this morning," Mrs Page said. "His father was on board the Hercules that was shot down yesterday in the Central Asian Republic. I'm sorry to tell you that David's father was the crew member who was killed."

A couple of gasps.

Then silence.

Woody put his head in his hands. He'd imagined a thousand times how it might feel to be woken in the night to be told his own dad was missing or killed. It was unthinkable. Unspeakable. He wondered how David would be feeling now. And he had a sister, Woody remembered. How would she be feeling? And his mum? Woody couldn't even begin to imagine.

"Lessons will go on as normal," Mrs Page said into the silence. "Our thoughts are with David and his family. But it is best that school continues."

Woody worked his way through a bowl of cereal, surrounded by his school-mates. No one said a word. No one looked at anyone else. When he had finished, Woody went up to his dorm. He had ten minutes before form class.

He took out his iPad, sat by the window and called his dad on Skype. He knew there was no way his dad would be there. He knew there was no way his dad would answer. He would be working or sleeping.

Woody held his breath as Skype tried to connect.

There was no reply.

THIRTEEN

There was one week to go until the final of the
National Schools Trophy. It was a cool night
for another training session. Mr Johnson was
driving the boys hard with complex passing
drills and fitness work.

Woody found that he loved the intensity of
rugby. He didn't have a fear of being hit any
more – he wanted contact. There was nothing
he enjoyed more than picking up his pace with
the ball, trying to find a gap. If he was brought
down, he just got up, ready to go again.

After training, Mr Johnson and Mr Searle
asked the boys to sit in a circle on the pitch.
Steam rose above them as they sat and
stretched their legs out in front of them. The

floodlights from the pitch lit up some boys' faces and cast shadows across others.

"We've had a letter from Shadwell School," Mr Johnson said. "Our opponents in the final. It's something we need to talk about."

As Mr Johnson spoke, Woody noticed someone walking across the pitch towards them. The person looked ghostly with the lights of the school drive behind him.

"They've offered to forfeit the match." Mr Johnson paused. "To let us have the trophy uncontested." Another pause. "What do you think?"

"Accept," Jesse said. "Then we've won and we don't even have to show up. Who votes yes?"

Woody watched three or four hands go up.

Then a voice from behind the rugby coaches.

"Don't accept."

The team turned to see David standing there. He was back from his dad's funeral.

"David," Mr Johnson said. "Come and join us."

David walked into the centre of the circle.

"I heard what you were saying," he said. "About the letter, sir. We can't accept the offer. We have to play the final and win."

Woody watched David stare out into the dark. He'd stopped speaking. But nobody broke the silence.

"If we don't, it's like accepting we're weak," David said. "Because of what happened to my dad. Because we all know that's why they're offering to pull out. And we're not weak. We can't be weak."

FOURTEEN

"What's up, Rory?" Woody asked, as he woke up with a start.

Rory was leaving the dorm with a ball under his arm and a notebook in his hand. It was dawn. The day before the final.

"Going kicking," Rory whispered.

"You never rest," Woody said.

"I'm awake," Owen muttered from under his duvet.

Rory shrugged, then smiled.

"Can I come?" Woody asked. "I'll field for you."

"Me too?" Owen asked, sitting up.

"OK," Rory said. "Be ready in five. Both of you."

Out on the pitch, Rory lined up six penalties. Six thumps of the ball. Six through the posts. Perfect.

Woody nodded to himself. He was impressed by Rory's skill, his dedication. Then he turned his mind to his own game. "Can we practise grubber kicks?" he asked. "I want to try something out."

"Sure," Rory agreed.

Woody tried a couple of times to break between Owen and Rory, as they stood between him and the try line. But it didn't really work. On his third attempt, Woody ended up running shoulder to shoulder with Owen, laughing,

hoofing the ball towards the posts at the near end of Luxton Park.

Neither boy heard Rory's warning as Woody pushed ahead of Owen to volley the ball underneath the posts, football style.

Woody heard barking first. Then a shout.

"YOU BOYS! GET OFF THE PARK! COME HERE!"

A volley of words, loud and hard. It could only be Mr Searle.

All three boys froze, their feet firmly on the out-of-bounds pitch.

When Mr Searle arrived, he snatched the ball from Owen.

"All three of you," he snapped. "Don't even start with the excuses. There's nothing you can say. Soccer on Luxton Park? I've never … I can't … You're all off the team. No final. No

Twickenham. Get out of my sight. I need to speak to Mr Johnson, right now."

Woody, Owen and Rory slouched back towards school. They had gone from the best of feelings to the worst. Now they felt nothing but shame and deep disappointment.

None of them spoke. What could they say?

FIFTEEN

It was the morning of the final, 24 hours later. There was a knock at the dorm door. The three boys groaned.

In the end, Woody answered it. He didn't want to face this. This was the day he was meant to play at Twickenham. The day he was going to make his dad proud. And he'd blown it.

Mr Johnson stood in the doorway. "The bus leaves at 9 o'clock sharp," he said. "I want you on it. OK?"

The three boys stared at the coach. They'd not seen him since before the incident on Luxton Park. A summons to the team bus wasn't what they'd been expecting. They'd been expecting fury.

"OK?" the coach asked.

"Yes, sir," Woody, Owen and Rory said, as one.

"I'll speak to Mr Searle. You think about the game. Sharpish. Do you want this or not?"

"We want it, sir!"

The bus was a proper coach, with decent heaters, a toilet and leg room. The team piled on, along with some of the teachers. Woody watched from the back seat. There was a lot to take in.

Mr Johnson was talking to a sullen Mr Searle.

David was sitting near the front, staring out stony-faced at the rain.

Jesse sat three rows away from his friend.

Woody tried to ignore his feelings towards Jesse and Mr Searle. If he let himself, he could get angry about them, but he didn't want to feel like that.

Woody wanted to focus on playing rugby. If he could get past everything he'd had to put up with in the last few days – as well as his anger – and just play rugby, that would be a victory in itself.

Twickenham towered over the school bus as it turned into the car park. Massive stands. England flags. A giant statue of a line-out – five rugby players leaping for the ball. And there were five words engraved around its base. Teamwork. Respect. Enjoyment. Discipline. Sportsmanship.

All chat had stopped as the bus drove through the streets of outer London. But now there was something more than silence.

It was awe.

That was what Woody was feeling. Jaw-dropping, eye-popping awe. To think that they were going to play here. And not only that – they were playing for the National Schools Trophy. If they won, they would qualify for the next level – the European Schools Trophy. Mr Johnson had told them about that part before, but it hadn't seemed real to Woody until now.

They walked in through the players' entrance past a huge St George's flag and into one of the dressing rooms, where they put their kitbags down on the floor.

Each player had their own place – a piece of card with their name and number above where their shirt was hanging.

On top of Woody's socks and shorts, there was an envelope.

A note from his dad.

'Woody. I'm proud of you beyond words. But words will have to do.

I'm sorry I'm not there with you today. I'll be watching online.

Love Dad.'

SIXTEEN

Walking out through the tunnel at Twickenham was like a dream. The perfect bright pitch. The bounce of the turf beneath their feet. The noise of the crowd, even though there were only 2,000 people in a stadium built for 82,000.

None of it felt real. Woody was struggling to cope with the scale of the stadium and the match he was about to take part in.

Borderlands versus Shadwell. The final of the National Schools Trophy.

On the pitch, Mr Johnson got the players into a huddle before kick-off.

"I want you to focus," he said. "We've worked on this. You are not to think of it as Twickenham until the game is over. This is just a rectangle of grass. A rugby pitch. OK?"

Woody said "OK" like the rest of the boys. But he knew he wasn't focused. There was too much to take in. The size of the stands. The huge blue sky. The sense of history.

And that lack of focus showed once the game kicked off. It was passing Woody by. Passing all the Borderlands team by. They were losing the key plays. They were making mistakes all over the pitch. Giving away points.

And then Woody took a short pass and knocked on. He heard the referee's whistle and David screaming at him at the same time. Right in his face.

"What the hell are you doing?" David yelled. "A knock-on from that. You're a joke."

Scrum to Shadwell.

From the scrum, Shadwell won a penalty. The Shadwell kicker stepped up and scored. 12–0.

The game was slipping away from Borderlands. Fast.

Then it got worse. At the next play, the Shadwell full back took the ball and charged through two Borderlands tackles. In desperation, David dived at the full back, taking him round the neck and both of them spinning to the ground.

After the pushing and shoving between both teams, the referee pulled out a card.

Yellow.

David was sin-binned. Eight minutes to half-time. Down to 14 players.

By the break it was 22–0.

The Twickenham dream was becoming a Twickenham nightmare.

Half-time.

David burst into the dressing room a minute after his team-mates had sat down. Mr Johnson stood at the centre of the room, hands on hips, overseeing a minute of silence before he spoke. He stepped back a little when David came in.

"Can I speak, sir?" David asked.

Mr Johnson hesitated. It was clear he was torn between anger that David had been sin-binned and reduced the team to 14 players, and the fact that his father had just been killed while serving his country. At last Mr Johnson nodded.

David's face was pink, his eyes red-rimmed, his voice loud and sharp. "That was pathetic," he said. "And I was the worst of us. I'm in the sin bin. Those last ten points? My fault. But you lot – all of you – are letting each other down. And the school down. And Mr Johnson down. What the ..."

David paused. "Can I swear, sir?"

Mr Johnson shook his head.

"What are we doing?" David went on, without drawing breath. "Our heads are in the clouds. Aren't we clever to be playing at Twickenham? No – we're not. I'll be ashamed to tell my family – or anyone else – about this. And you should all be ashamed. Sitting there. You make me sick. I make myself sick ..."

Woody watched David as he ran out of words. Out of anger. He looked close to tears. The days of grief he'd endured were written across his face.

Then Owen stood up. He just stood up and looked at David. No words.

David nodded at Owen.

Next Rory stood up.

Then a couple of the backs, Thomas and Rahim.

Woody followed, standing too.

There was something moving through the room now. Something unspoken. Something that had changed the mood. Woody could feel the hairs prickling on the back of his neck and on his arms.

Now the whole team was standing up and looking at David. Silent. But with him.

David glanced at Mr Johnson.

Mr Johnson smiled. "Lead them out, David."

The second half was going to be different. Woody could tell that as soon as Shadwell School kicked off to restart the game. The mood of the Borderlands players changed everything. David had stirred their passion for the match.

There was now a force to Borderlands' game – an unstoppable force that began to work its magic four minutes into the second half. It was the first scrum after the break. Woody saw that the Borderlands pack were pushing twice as hard, using all their weight. It caught the Shadwell pack by surprise and they turned too fast, leaving three of their players offside.

Penalty.

The first kickable penalty for Rory, who went through his calm routine of focusing his body and his mind before he stepped up.

22–3.

Over the next 30 minutes, Borderlands earned five more penalties. Shadwell School were making more and more errors. They were rattled by Rory. And now they had seen him in action, they knew he was deadly with his foot and any mistake they made could be punished by three points.

And deadly he was. Six from six. The score was 22–18. Five minutes to go.

Shadwell restarted, kicking the ball high at an angle instead of deep into Borderlands territory, trying to keep it in their own possession.

Woody thought it was a mis-kick at first and he wasn't sure what to do. He stooped and picked up the ball. Except he didn't. He fumbled it. And stumbled. And the ball spun away. And Woody heard the whistle.

Knock-on. His second of the game. Scrum to Shadwell well into the Borderlands half.

Woody knew he'd blown it. Borderlands needed possession to have any chance of scoring the five points they needed to win.

Now Shadwell had the ball. Woody could see the grins on the faces of the opposition. They'd been under the kosh – but now they could win it by holding onto the ball.

The clock was running down. Two minutes to go. And then, at last, the ball broke – a fumble from a Shadwell player this time. Nerves on both sides. Woody scrambled for the ball, his first touch since his knock-on.

He bent to take it. He had to get this right. He looked about him. Who to pass to? There was no one. And the Shadwell defenders were almost on top of him.

So Woody dropped the ball onto his foot and kicked it, a grubber kick that spun between three advancing Shadwell players. Then he used every bit of muscle he had to power his body through the defence.

When Woody broke through their line, he caught up with the ball ahead of him and booted it harder, gaining speed all the time.

Woody was in his element. He was running. He was in control of a ball. He felt that nothing could stop him.

The Shadwell lines were in disarray.

His third kick came after he had broken through the forwards.

He had clear ground now.

He could hear the Shadwell forwards shouting behind him. But he believed in his pace.

Over the halfway line. 30 metres out. Woody tried to get his boot under the ball for his fourth kick.

The ball bounced, reared up. He had it. 15 metres out.

In the next second, Woody saw two Shadwell players converging on him. And a flash of yellow and blue to his left.

A Borderlands shirt.

Jesse. Ten metres wide.

Woody felt the first Shadwell player's hand take his waist. But as he began to go down, he off-loaded the ball to his left, spinning it hard.

The ball went straight into the arms of Jesse.

Jesse was eight metres out. He dodged a last, desperate Shadwell tackle, then dived for the line.

Try.

Right under the posts.

Woody was aware of some tension in the crowd now. Would Borderlands convert the try? But Woody smiled. He knew that Rory would never miss the kick from there.

A pause. Then Rory stepped up to kick.

And scored.

The game was over. Borderlands had won. They were National Schools Champions.

Woody looked over at the crowd. Some of them were shouting and cheering, others just clapping – all of them on their feet, all of them caught up in the game. And he saw Mr Johnson and Mr Searle dancing on the edge of the pitch.

Then Woody saw David run over to the side of the seating. There was a woman and a girl there. They must be his mum and sister. Woody saw David's sister leap into his arms. The two of them staggered around, half laughing and half crying. There was a sad smile on their mum's face.

Now Woody felt even happier. For David and his family. Their moment of happiness made this win even more of a good thing.

SEVENTEEN

Back in the dorm at Borderlands, Woody flicked on Skype. It was a reflex now. Something he did. Just in case. But – as ever – he knew the chances of his dad being there were one in a thousand.

"Hi, Woody."

Woody nearly fell off his bed. There was his dad's face, close to the camera.

"Dad! Are you OK? What can you tell me?"

"I'm fine, son. Things have calmed down a bit. Let's say I'm getting a bit more time on the ground."

Woody grinned. His dad was safe. That made him feel better than anything. Better than lifting the silver trophy at Twickenham. But he still couldn't wait to tell him about the game.

"I know why you're grinning," his dad said.

"You're OK," Woody said, puzzled. "That's why."

Woody's dad smiled. "I watched a rugby match this afternoon," he said.

"Yeah?"

"Yeah," his dad said. "It was pretty good. There was this centre playing. He was a natural ... er ... footballer."

Woody grinned again, fell back on his bed and began to tell his dad about the match and the news that Borderlands were going to Toulon to play for the European Schools Trophy and that he might be in the team.

"So, what about our deal, Woody?" his dad asked.

"Deal?" Woody asked, although he knew exactly what his dad was talking about.

"About you staying at Borderlands. Until after the war?"

"The deal's still on, Dad."

"Just until I get back?" his dad said. "Then you can choose – football or rugby."

"We'll see, Dad," Woody said. He'd been trying hard not to, but now his face finally cracked into a big smile. A smile that showed he was happy. A smile that showed he couldn't wait to play more rugby.

ACKNOWLEDGEMENTS

Thanks are due to my wife, my daughter, my agent. To Jim Sells, David Brayley, Tom Bonnett, Ali Taft, Anna Turner and James Nash. Also Duncan Wright and his colleagues at Stewart's Melville College. The children and teachers at Albrighton Primary School and the men and women of RAF Cosford. And to Barrington Stoke. Thank you!

Our books are tested
for children and young people by
children and young people.

Thanks to everyone who consulted on
a manuscript for their time and effort in
helping us to make our books better
for our readers.